If All the Animals Came Inside

by
ERIC PINDER

illustrated by
MARC BROWN

L B

Little, Brown and Company
New York • Boston

If all the animals came inside,
my brother would cry. My sister would hide.

The doggy would bark. The kitten would hiss.
My parents would make funny faces—like this!

But I wouldn't look for a place to hide.
I'd climb aboard for an elephant ride.

THUMP RHUMP.
BANG BUMP.

The walls would tremble. The windows would shake.
Oh, what a terrible mess we would make!

When all the animals played hide-and-seek,
I'd cover my eyes, but the monkeys would peek.
They'd laugh and they'd point. They'd swing and they'd run.
I'd hide with a hippo and have so much fun.

The walls would tremble. The closets would quake.
Oh, what a terrible mess we would make!

When all the animals wanted a snack,
the skunk and the panda and even the yak
would rush to the kitchen and chew up our food.
Mommy would tell them to stop being rude.

LUNCH MUNCH.
BURP CRUNCH.

The walls would tremble. The dishes would break.
Oh, what a terrible mess we would make!

When all the animals needed a drink,
they'd slobber and drool all over the sink.
The badger would blubber. The grizzly would burp.
My sister would mutter, "It's not nice to slurp!"

The walls would tremble. The cupboards would shake.
Oh, what a terrible mess we would make!

The lions would roar as they sprawled on the floor.
The lemurs would lollygag right by the door.
My daddy would try to sit down in his chair.
He'd holler and whoop with a porcupine there!

OW. WOW! OUCH. YOUCH!

The walls would tremble. The sofa would break.
Oh, what a terrible mess we would make!

The gibbons would giggle. Hyenas would laugh.
The ostrich and I would go race the giraffe.
We'd follow the bears as they ran up the stairs.
We'd bounce on the beds and knock over chairs!

RUMBLE JUMBLE. POUNCE BOUNCE.

The walls would tremble. The dressers would shake.
Oh, what a terrible mess we would make!

At bathtime my daddy would stammer and stare.
"You can't take a bath with an octopus there!"
The faucet would leak. The bathroom would flood.
Daddy would slip and he'd land with a thud!

SPLISH SPLASH.
SLIP SPLAT.

The walls would tremble. The toilet would shake.
Oh, what a terrible mess we would make!

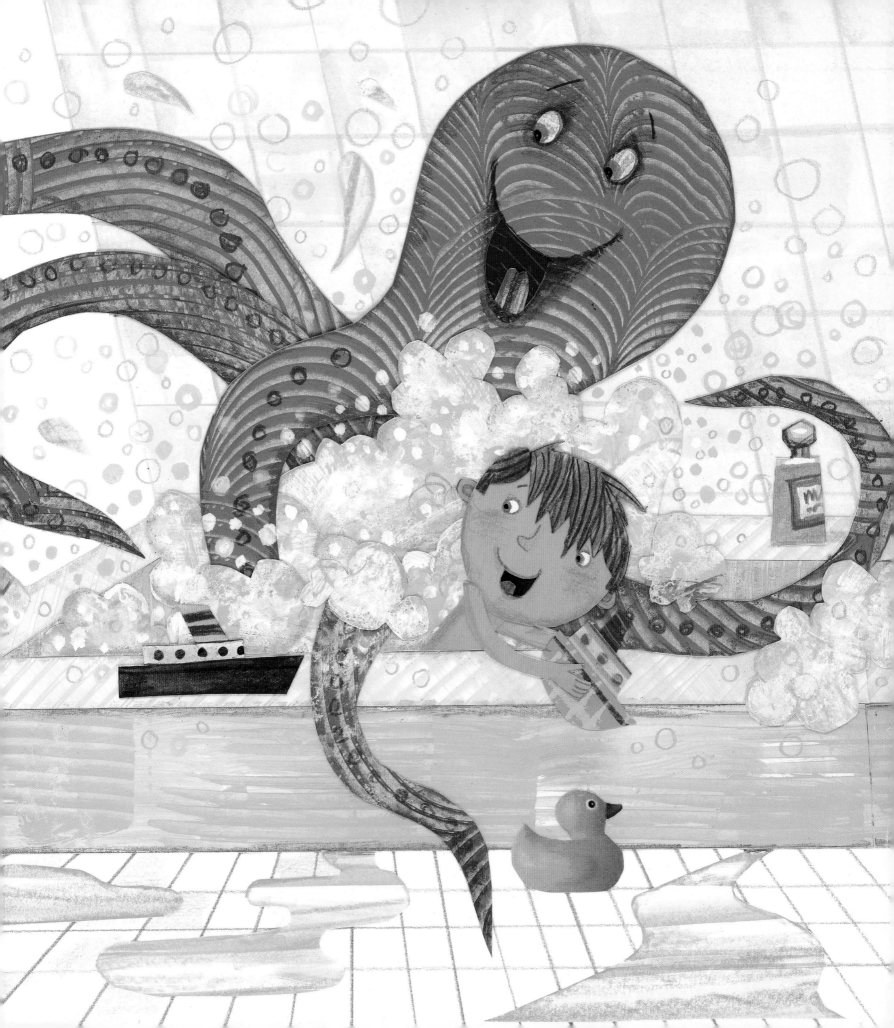

When all the animals wanted to play,
they'd grab all my toys. They'd take them away!
Upstairs and downstairs and out in the hall,
the chipmunks would draw with my paint on the wall.

Families!

WIBBLE SCRIBBLE.
WIPE SWIPE.

The walls would tremble. The crayons would break.
Oh, what a terrible mess they would make!

The bats would be dealing my cards on the ceiling.
The squirrels would be squealing. The paint would be peeling.

The rhinos downstairs would be watching TV.
They'd stand in the way and leave no room for me!

Spilling the popcorn and causing a riot,
whooping and snorting—they'd never be quiet!

Every last creature would sleep in my bed,
with oodles of pillows, one for each head.

From sunset to sunrise, the wolves and the owls
would keep us awake with their hooting and howls.

We'd have nowhere to sleep, so we'd stretch and we'd yawn.
We'd pack up our tent and go play on the lawn.

As fun as a house full of critters could be,
my dog and my kitten are plenty for me.

But oh, what a wild and wonderful ride
when all the animals came inside.

For Uma and the Schnookiemuffins:
Kate, Maha, Sarah, and Sylvia
—E.P.

For Laurie, my partner in paint and paper
—M.B.

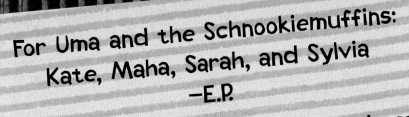

The art was cut from papers painted with gouache
and includes photographic elements.
The text was set in Skizzors.

Little, Brown and Company is a division of Hachette Book Group, Inc.
The Little, Brown name and logo are trademarks of Hachette Book Group, Inc.
The publisher is not responsible for websites (or their content) that are not owned by the publisher.
First Edition: April 2012

Library of Congress Cataloging-in-Publication Data
Pinder, Eric, 1970–
If all the animals came inside / by Eric Pinder ; illustrated by Marc Brown. — 1st ed.
p. cm.
Summary: Illustrations and rhyming text explore the
fun and mayhem that could ensue if elephants,
kangaroos, bats, and more were to come
inside a little boy's house.
ISBN 978-0-316-09883-0
[1. Stories in rhyme. 2. Animals—Fiction.]
I. Brown, Marc Tolon, ill. II. Title.
PZ8.3.P5586772If 2012
[E]—dc23
2011020100

10 9 8 7 6 5 4 3 2 1
IM
Printed in China